Barry Timms

Faye Hsu

Noah
and the
Starbird

LITTLE TiGER
LONDON

Noah sniffed and waved goodbye to Mum.
"Tell Daddy to get well soon," he called.
Granny's hug was warm and welcoming.
"The hospital will take good care of Daddy,"
she smiled. "And I'll take care of you."

Together they unpacked his clothes.
"Granny - what's that?" Noah asked.

"A lamp," she replied. "It was my
grandma's. I thought you might like it."
A little bird gleamed behind the glass.
It looked like it could flutter away.

At bedtime, the lamp glowed brightly.
"I think that bird is magic," whispered
Granny, kissing Noah goodnight.

Noah couldn't sleep. When would Daddy be home? Was he lonely in hospital?

Suddenly a flapping of feathers made Noah jump. It was the bird from the lamp!

"I'm the Starbird," she chirped. "And you must be Noah."

"I know you're worried," said the bird,
"but I promise your daddy is safe."
She sang a soft lullaby and Noah snuggled down.
"Thank you," he whispered. "I feel so
much better when you're here."

"Even the bravest of us need a little help,"
said the Starbird. She pulled from her tail
a shimmering feather. "To keep you strong,"
she chirped, and she flew out into the night.

Next morning, Noah told Granny his secret.
"I knew that bird was magic," she marvelled.
"What a special friend!"

Noah sat with Granny while she called Mum at the hospital.

"Daddy's still no better, love," said Granny at last. "We'll have to be patient."

Noah sighed. How he missed Daddy's hugs.

"Let's take the Starbird into the garden,"
said Granny, leading Noah outside.
At once, all the birds flew down,
chirping and flapping with joy.
"They like your new friend!" Granny laughed.

When darkness fell, the Starbird fluttered to life.

"I miss my daddy," Noah said sadly.

"Tell me about him," cheeped the bird.

"He swings me so high I could touch
the stars!" Noah beamed.

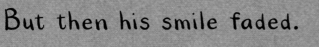

But then his smile faded.

"Be brave if you can," the bird tweeted softly. "I'll be close by."

"I'll try," said Noah. He held the magic feather tight and drifted off to sleep.

But the next morning Daddy was still
poorly. Granny hugged Noah close.
"We'll both have to be strong," she said.
"Then we'll need my magic feather,"
Noah decided.

Granny fetched her crafting box.
"Let's keep busy and make
a picture," she smiled.
    "Of a bird!" cheered Noah.
    They filled the afternoon
with buttons and beads,
glitter and glue.

That evening, Noah had an idea.

"Daddy needs this feather to make
him brave," he told the Starbird.
"I'd like to give it to him — but how?"

"Together we might do it,"
she chirped. Then she flew
around him, sprinkling
stardust, till Noah
floated high above
the floor.

"I can fly!"
he gasped.

They rushed to the window.
"What if I fall?" Noah worried,
looking down.

"Remember your courage," said the
Starbird. And with a hop
and a flutter . . .

. . . they flew into a starlit night.
 High above the clouds they soared, over
mountains and forests, cities and rivers.

"The hospital!" cried Noah.
"Over there! We did it!"
   Down they both swooped.

And there through the window
was the face that Noah's heart so
longed for. "Daddy!" he beamed.

Quiet as a midnight cloud, Noah slipped
the feather under Daddy's pillow.
"It's yours now," he whispered.

It was a long way back to Granny's house.
Even the Starbird seemed less bright
when at last Noah climbed into bed.

Morning came. Breakfast time passed.
And still Noah snoozed.

Then Granny's voice was calling his name.
"Wake up, sleepyhead," she gushed.
"Mum phoned! Daddy's better!"
"Hooray!" cheered Noah.

Soon it was time to say goodbye.
"Please light the lamp each night,
Granny," Noah smiled. "Others might
need the Starbird's help."
Then Daddy scooped him up
in a big, warm hug. And
Noah felt like he could
touch the stars.